Eggtooth
Solla Carrock

Running Girl Press

Portland, Oregon

2013

First Printing

First Published in 2013

Copyright 2013 Solla Carrock

Printed in the U.S.A.

Published by

Running Girl Press

Portland, Oregon

info@runninggirlpress.com

Front cover drawing: *Birth* by Solla Carrock

ISBN 978-0-9888292-1-3

Acknowledgments

I would like to thank Erin Carrock, Anna Shook and the Portland Novel group of Carol Collier, Leanne McLennon and Mark Anderson for reading, editing, advice and support.

An eggtooth is a temporary tooth or (in birds) projection of the beak used for piecing the eggshell. Using it the animal makes its way out of the shell in a few hours which also gives it a change to gradually adjust to the world outside the shell.

Forest

I am here in the forest. The forest is everything, but according to the stories it was not always everything and everywhere. It may not be this way for you. So I will tell you about it as if the forest was a stranger, as if you did not know it as I do like the back of my hand. In other words, not at all, so familiar I don't really look.

If you looked for the first time, this is what you would see:

Trees everywhere. Nowhere that you can see more than five or six feet without a tree growing, except where they have been deliberately cut away, and then they grow back quickly and have to be cut and cut away again.

There are a few trees that are what we call the old forest. Those trees are thick. Their bark is hard, black, and, in the cracks, the color of dirt. Most of these trees are still not so big that you cannot reach around them and clasp your hands on the other side. Just a few are, the oldest of those from the old time, long before anyone who lives now was born. Some of those have branches low enough that you can get up in the tree, in the great hollow formed by branches coming together in the center. You feel held, cradled there, by this tree. These are the trees that we revere, and yet they hold us, so gentle, so safe.

But I have been speaking as though you could see, like I can. But if you did not know this forest, if you were coming here for the first time, suddenly just here in the forest, quite likely you would not be able to see with your eyes so used to light.

I have seen the light. We all do in the time of our rasha, the journey from the dark of the forest, to the light of the sun shore. But we do not travel quickly from dark into light, or light into dark. At the very edges of the great world we live in, not all the world - I know that now - but all the world that we know, there is a thin strip of sand where no trees grow, where nothing grows. It is bare to the sky and coming out into it is a frightening thing, which we might never do except for our need that comes in the time of rasha. Our need then is so strong it takes us over, like strong drink, like falling in love. And even so, even though we have labored for days, frenzied, to break our way out of the forest, when we finally come near the edge we cringe within the shelter of the last dwindling trees.

During that time our eyes adjust. But we do not think of it as getting used to the light, but rather as facing our fear of the light.

Coming back, we are full. We enter slowly back into the world, into forest. We do not notice as our eyes open again to darkness. We are simply coming home.

Rashas don't come often. Three times before a girl is as tall as she ever will be and a boy is nearly as tall as he will ever be. Another time before the girl is a woman of an age to bear children. Four more times before her first child is grown. Another four before she is old, but still strong and healthy. Another rasha and her age begins to slow her down. The next and she might die during her time on the beach. For a few death comes the next time or the time after that.

But I am Mayak, long lived one, an old man now, and I have traveled seventeen rashas. Another will come soon and I think it will be the last. But there is something I must do first.

Telling you of the forest is not what I must do, but it clears out the undergrowth in my mind.

Most of the forest is not made of the old trees with the hard bark. Most of the trees are thin and brittle shooting up as quickly as they can to reach a piece of the sky. A single one would not even bear your weight, but packed so closely together and even crossing and re-crossing each other like a net, sometimes the tree branches form a structure that you can climb.

Also weaving in and out among them are vines. The vines grow over them and around them, reach to the top of them, and along with the leaves on branches that suddenly spread wide from the tree as it goes high enough to reach clear sky, the vines also cover the top of our world, so there is barely any blue for us to see. What we do see is rather like the stars that come out at night on the beach. Those stars at night that flicker are like the little bits of blue in the forest during the daytime.

On the forest floor as well, the vines grow to fill up all the spaces, but down below we walk through it and bend it back. We hack at it with our knives. We build houses, not to protect us from the open air, but to hold some place clear for us, to keep the wall of vines from closing in.

If I imagine it not being like this, if I remember those times on the beach walking with nothing touching me, this is what I imagine you would notice, something always brushing against you, touching you, tickling you, and you always ducking and shoving to make your way.

Here I am in the forest, surrounded by tree branches, vines, hanging fruits, small insects that dart in the small spaces. Here I came to pick the kala berries for little Soshi and stopped to rest in the thick of the forest, near to the farther clearing. I was hidden here within a clump of vine, though I was not hiding, but merely standing where I came to rest.

3

This was what I saw in this spot where I was not seen.

Atoya came into the clearing. Daughter's daughter's son.

Atoya paced, back and forth, almost back and forth. Many times he stumbled and lost even that direction. Atoya, going nowhere.

Atoya

Atoya's legs were like bird's legs, thin stalks. That's how they felt to me, though when I forced myself to really look, I could see they were no thinner than those of most children. It was only his strange tiptoe walk, often off-balance, that gave the impression of frailty.

"He will keep the forest floor clear for us." I said the words, as I always said them, and indeed only constant use kept the forest from creeping back into our dwelling places and our paths. But it was only to comfort myself, to give purpose to what had no purpose.

It was so hard to watch. What made it harder for me was how I could see Tala in the boy. It was something in the structure of the bones of his face. Tala, too, had been thin, so spare he seemed fragile. But Tala's thinness had the suppleness of a young vine, while there was something brittle about Atoya.

"They're nothing the same," I said to myself.

Then a look of fright flittered across Atoya's face. It was Tala's look, a look I remembered from so long ago. He was young when the Sun took him, my first love, father to my daughter. He had that look of sudden fright. Moments later it would change to laughter. I had often wondered about that look, what he'd been thinking. But I never asked. I don't know why I never asked. Perhaps it unnerved me, Tala frightened. Tala was the brave one. He was the one who had left his group and followed me home to mine. He didn't even ask me if I would go with him instead. He saw me looking toward my path, looking back at him, torn, and he simply strode up.

"Wait for me," he said, "I must say goodbye."

It would not take long, with the path already clear. Soon he was beside me again.

"Let's go," he said. That walk back, did my feet even touch the ground? I felt as if my soul still soared to the Sun, and it was all I could do to make one step at a time instead of flying. I remember reaching back for his hand, and how he took mine so firmly. Skin to my skin, it held me and let me walk.

Now I wondered if Tala's moments of fright were just all the strangeness gathering up and coming on him unawares. He had walked with me away from mother, fathers, brothers, sisters, clan, his nana and poppas, all those who hold us within, who gather us to them and remind us of who we are.

Of course, that was why people usually partnered within their own group. Only a few brave ones, like Tala, venture outward. I wondered sometimes if I should have asked it of him - but I hadn't asked. He hadn't made me. And the look never lasted more than a moment, and then he laughed, as though he felt the Sun within him and everywhere around him. His eye would catch mine. Every time it did, my spirit flew, and I was home. I think it was the same for him. I hope it was.

He was so different, my Tala, and yet, each time I looked at Atoya, I could see Tala within.

But, with Atoya, it was not just a moment of fright, a moment when everything seemed unfamiliar. In Atoya, it seemed the strangeness was always there, the difference, the aloneness, the hand that never seemed to grasp firmly.

I looked from my hidden place, and I felt pain. I thought, "When have I looked at you without pain?"

Birth

Atoya had been born during the visit of the messengers. I still think of them as the messengers from the Sun, though now I doubt that they came from the Sun at all, or even knew much at all of the true Sun beyond the globe that shines in the sky.

Yet they overwhelmed me once. Not right at first. Indeed, at first I was shocked at their sacrilege, for they all came tramping out of Sari's sun path, a whole group of them, and Sari not yet returned. Did they all mean to partner with Sari then, having walked his sun path home? Why did they all have so many clothes, and such odd looking ones?

Then I noticed their pale skin, so white what forest light there was reflected off it. They were so tall they had to bend to even come through the path. Perhaps they were spirits rather than men. But no, they emerged from the path, saw me, and spoke. They said they were men, and they spoke in the language of men, though their words came out oddly, not sounding quite right. It was a struggle to understand at first, but I got used to it.

When they told me they had come from another world in another part of the sky, I thought that perhaps they were from the land of the Sun and so blessed they might walk any path they chose. But looking them over, I doubted it. They were so gawky and awkward, too tall and too big.

The tallest of them, who also looked the youngest, said, "Hi, I'm Loren." He reached out and broke off a twig. He pulled off strips of bark as he talked.

"One of us came before," he said. "He stayed with a group of people on this island. Maybe you heard something about him?"

I nodded. I'd heard of the man Loren must be speaking of. It had been a very long time ago. A woman who had lain with me during my sun time told me of a man who had come alone to their group. At first, he had spoken in words they didn't understand. I remembered this now, although I hadn't thought about it in a long time. The woman told me about how tall the man was, and how pale, and how strange even when he had learned to speak as people do. He had stayed awhile and then gone. One of the people who had been on the sun shore when he left claimed to have woken from sun trance and seen him stepping into a large hut that rose up towards the Sun. Most of her tribe had taken this for a sun vision, but she'd said she wasn't so sure.

So, I looked at the men and decided, yes, surely they were blessed by the Sun.

"Did he stay with you then?" the young man asked. I shook my head and explained. We didn't talk much more then. It was late, nearly time for sleep.

"Would it be okay if we stayed with your group for awhile?" asked an older man. He held out his hand, and said, "I'm Eduardo."

I took his hand, but it was somewhat stiff. I laughed awkwardly, I suppose because it was odd, his offering me his touch, but then seeming so ill at ease with it, and saying it like that, "my group".

"It's not my group," I said, "but you are welcome. The forest welcomes all. There is no need to ask."

They held back. Maybe they didn't understand why I laughed. "You'll need some beds," I said, and led them to a clear place. They seemed to be having trouble seeing though the darkness was not yet deep. I bent down a couple of saplings and starting pulling off vines and thin branches from other trees to weave between them. I hadn't intended to build their beds, but they seemed at a loss, just standing about.

Suddenly one of them pulled something from out of his clothing and it lit up the forest where it pointed.

It took me by surprise. "The Sun," I shouted, "how have you brought it?" Of course, it was not, nothing like, not even that bright. It lit only a very small space. It was just so startling in contrast with the dark of the forest, and the suddenness. How could even a bit of the Sun come here in the middle of the forest? It had never happened before.

No one answered my question, but Eduardo angrily grabbed the arm of the man who held the light. He took the thing that made the light and did something to it that made the light stop.

"It's okay," he told me.

I got over it, and went back to helping them with their beds. They seemed to be getting the hang of it now. They didn't need so much help. Every once in awhile, I'd try to look at them without their noticing. Who were they, entrusted with light? Were they indeed sent by the Sun? But I didn't ask. I was scared, I think, but I don't know of what. When the work was done, I left for my own bed.

It was the next evening that Nochi's labor began. I was talking with Loren when she began to pull down vines and harok bushes. So, I knew my great grandchild had begun the journey out of the dark forest of her womb.

"What's she doing? Loren asked me.

"She's building a hut for the birthing," I explained. There were so many things the messengers seemed to know nothing of. Of course, they might make beds differently, but it was strange that they didn't know how children were born.

Another messenger looked distressed, "I'm a doctor. She shouldn't be doing that. She ought to lie down and rest."

"Doctor," was that his name, but why did he offer it as an explanation? Why should Nochi lie down now, when it was so early? She'd only be restless, waiting with nothing to do.

"It's what we always do," I felt troubled. Could it be wrong?

Doctor saw me hesitate. He insisted, "That kind of work could make the baby come too soon, or tear her inside so the baby won't live through the birth." His voice was kindly and concerned, and urgent. He seemed so sure. Sometimes babies did die. Could that be why? I felt confused, almost dazed. The mother always built the hut, preparing a place for the child to be born into. How could he ask Nochi not to do so? Yet, if they came from the Sun?

Doctor waited, watched me. I ran to Kalak, Nochi's partner, and told him what Doctor had said. Then he talked with Nochi. She looked at the strangers with suspicion, but she agreed. She had been close by the night before. She had seen the light.

Kalak and I built the hut instead. It didn't take long. Thin branches and vines broke easily. We hurried all the more seeing Nochi stand there restlessly, holding herself back from her need to build a haven, her black eyes darting over at the strangers. We stuffed grasses into the remaining gaps. There, finished. I was relieved. Now she could rest easy.

Once we went inside, Nochi laid down as Doctor told her, but I could see that she was impatient and would likely jump up again soon. Then Doctor brought out one of those things that make a light. For a moment I was blinded, it lit up the small hut so brightly. Then joy surged through me. These messengers had come to allow my grandchild to be born into the light. It filled me with pride, too, wondering what kind of special child was going to be born. And now, Nochi laid back, overwhelmed for once, and she made no protest when Doctor spoke to her. None of us protested, all of us were so in awe of these strangers. We followed Doctor's directions. He surely, we thought, knew more of the ways of the Sun. He sent us all away, me, and all the fathers except Kalak. Kalak could be with her until the actual birth when he would be in the way, Doctor said.

This was not our way. Our way is to surround the mother, to support her, and to be there when the baby made its way out. I was uneasy with it, yet I accepted it. I told myself that Kalak would call us back if he felt the need. I stayed close, just outside the hut. I talked some, quietly, with the other strangers. Other friends and family were nearby, shy of the strangers, so they didn't come too close. After a time, the strangers went off to their beds, and Micah and Reaza came to sit with me. At some point I fell asleep. I woke a few times in the night, but all was quiet, the others asleep on the ground beside me.

All the next day Kalak and Nochi stayed alone in the hut, with Kalak coming out occasionally for food, and Doctor going in. Normally, I would have come and gone, knowing that others were also coming and going into and out of the hut, letting Nochi and the baby to come know they were there. Now, instead, we were all outside, waiting, uneasy. Waiting made the time grow tiresome. The messengers also tired me. They seemed so ill at ease, impatient, continually glancing beyond the clearing to where the forest grew thick, or above their head where branches and vines wove a dense roof. Watching them, I couldn't help feeling closed in.

The air felt hot and thick, though it was the same as always. Once Loren grinned over at me.

"How can you stand it, all these bugs?"

His question surprised me, "They're always here," I answered. "They don't bother me."

The other fathers sat in the clearing and watched the hut, since they weren't allowed to be with the mother, or restlessly chopped a new path through the thick brush of jungle on the pretext of finding some delicacy that Nochi particularly favored.

I worried about Nochi, left without their support, but she did have Kalak, and, of course, the messenger and the light. No, the fathers were worse off, left with no one to soothe. Many other people, too, had gathered in the clearing to stare at the messengers. They had heard about the light. But few of them said anything.

As the day progressed, Doctor became more and more agitated. I didn't know what was wrong. Finally he came up to me. I was tending a fat brown baby whose mother had gone for a moment of solace to a private place in the forest. The baby held herself upright by grasping my fingers.

Doctor stared at her for a moment. "She's strong," he said, but it was as if he barely saw her.

Then he burst out with, "It's taking too long. She's barely dilated. The contractions just aren't strong enough, and I've got no rititocin to speed it along."

"Rititocin?"

"It's a drug...a medicine, to speed up the birth."

"Why would you want to do such a thing? The baby will come in its own time."

"That's what we used to think, that there was no harm in a long labor. But now we know that it doesn't usually take so long unless something is going wrong with the labor, and the baby can be harmed."

It had not even been so long, but I felt his fear spread through me. I tried to calm myself so I could talk with him, but Doctor got up abruptly, swiping irritably at a vine that hung down from the canopy. He only said, as he left, "If it isn't born soon, something should be done."

That night Kalak woke me from a deep sleep, "Doctor wants you."

"Oh, why?" I turned over and struggled to drag myself away from sleep.

"He wants to do something to bring the birth. I told him I needed to talk to you and the other fathers and Nochi."

"What do you think?" I asked him.

Kalak looked down and awkwardly shook his head. "They make you so afraid," he said. His face struggled; I could see he wanted to word it just right. "Sometimes children fall from trees," he said. "Sometimes babies are born without breath. It is hard. It hurts. But we aren't always afraid of it. Now I feel afraid, as if I'm expecting the bad things." Then he got shy and didn't say any more for a while. Then he said, "I just can't remember if the babies who

13

didn't live took longer to be born like Doctor says. I don't think so, but I can't say for sure."

I too, had been trying to remember. I nodded at him.

Then he went to fetch the others and we all gathered near the entrance to the hut. Doctor came out.

It was taking way too long, Doctor explained, dangerously long. The baby needed to be cut out. He explained how the cut would be mended again so no harm would come to the mother.

"How can this be so?" I still didn't feel completely awake. I had been deep into sleep. And it felt odd out here with these men talking about what might happen to my granddaughter's body.

It would be a birth without the birthing journey. That would be like going to the Sun without first having to cut your way out of the forest. How could it be? But they were from the Sun. Perhaps the Sun had sent the messengers for this reason, to see the child safely born. "Thus the Sun watches over each of us." I felt proud suddenly, as I thought of the special destiny the Sun must have in mind for my great grandchild that the baby need not even struggle out, but could be lifted out direct from the womb to the light.

So, I didn't argue against it. Kalak and I went inside with Doctor who explained it to Nochi. Her look questioned me, but seeing my feelings, she agreed. She was very quiet, perhaps from the birthing, or from all the time in the light.

Doctor asked Kalak to leave, but he asked me to stay and help him. I was awake now. It was so bright. He told me how everything had to stay very clean so there would be no infection.

"Infection?"

When he explained it sounded very like a narok bush scratch when it swelled and burned the body. So, I scrubbed with his special water and tied a cloth over my face, like Doctor did. He spoke gently to Nochi, telling her he was going to give her something to sleep, and when she woke the baby would be there to see.

How quickly she slept. And then Doctor seemed in a hurry so everything happened very quickly. I expected blood from the cutting, but Doctor did something to stop it as he cut. I couldn't see just what he did. Perhaps it was because of all the light that made me want to shut my eyes and rise to the Sun. Then there was the baby being lifted out and handed to me to hold. At first it lay in my arms all blue and limp, like another baby I'd seen once that hadn't made it out of the womb, and was pushed out finally. But moving quickly Doctor cleaned its mouth and nose and moved its limbs about a little, and almost at once the baby breathed and cried.

At first I felt relief as I watched the tiny body go from blue to reddish. But I breathed in sharply as I listened to this baby cry. The cry was peculiar, painful. It grated. I've heard the cries of many newborn babies. All of a sudden the baby has thrust itself out of the passageway into air and onto dirt or a pair of hands. Its cry is a sound of shocked surprise, before it collects itself and takes a look around at the larger world. This was not like that. It sounded nervous, almost wounded. I stood there awkwardly holding this baby who cried such a cry, but Doctor seemed pleased.

"A boy," he said, before he turned to cut the cord and sew up the wound he had made.

As there was no nursing to comfort the baby, I did the best I could, holding him close and rocking my body.

15

It was a relief when Kalak stuck his head in, "Can we come in?"

I pulled him through the door, and handed the baby over to him. Doctor frowned but said nothing. Later he came over to examine the baby. He looked surprised when he saw the pads on the baby's hands and knees and toes. He felt their suctioning. "I've never seen anything like this before."

Now I was surprised, and scared. He helped a child to be born and he knew nothing about even this basic thing. Perhaps where he came from all babies were lifted out of the womb and had no need of them. I said, "They help the baby to make its way out."

He reached for my hands, and turned them palm up, "But you haven't got them."

"Oh, no. They drop off after a few days." Then Doctor looked troubled, but said nothing. Yet the baby crying, still crying, hadn't bothered him. What could be worse than that?

Later when Nochi woke, nursing was difficult for the baby. Everything seemed tortuous for him those first days. I hoped that it was only that for such a child of the Sun the ways of the forest were difficult and strange. I told myself he would learn quickly. But instead he continued to cry. I was glad of his many fathers, for none of them, nor even his mother, could stand to be with him for long. Often, after they had handed the baby off to another, one of them would rush off quickly and I could hear him hacking a path through the forest with almost as much energy as if he were in rasha. I found myself doing the same. The baby's crying filled me with a fretfulness that needed release.

Light

The next day we had the celebration, as always, but it was not as always. Still, some things were the same. His mother held the newborn, while all his fathers huddled round her to lend their support. And round them, all the others of our tribe. The fathers took their turns at taking the babe and holding him up to be seen by those near him, as I chanted the old words, of the story of how we came to be reborn in this place.

Once the people lived in the light, but did not know the light, for light was all there was. So Sun caused the forest to spring forth. The trees grew gigantic, spreading forth their huge bowers to shut out the light. The vines sprang forth growing over the spaces between the branches so the light was dimmed and the people were shadows. The people feared, but Sun pitied them and opened their eyes wider so they could see in the dimness.

Sun told them, "When you hunger for me, you shall find me." So the people had hope. They no longer feared what they could not see, and they were content in their waiting. Not yet did they reach for the Sun. They wished for the light, but not yet the true light, so they felt the dimness to be almost as good.

Then one day one of them felt the hunger for the Sun. It was Nolak, a woman. Seeing her, Kiriac too felt the hunger. Then they understood that the shadow world was not the light, and the light was more than the light that they had known of old. They heard the Sun calling. They went to the Sun, knowing the way through the bushes and vines.

Sun gave Nolak and Kiriac strength to move through the forest, breaking their way though the growth of the forest floor, until they reached the sun shore.

There Nolak saw the light of the Sun become so bright it blinded her. She fell down on the burning sand. It pierced her through. When Kiriac gazed upward, the same thing happened to him. Their bodies lay senseless. They were with the Sun.

When they could see again they saw the Sun dancing through all things. It flickered on the small waves, the sand, the leaves of the mother forest. When they looked at each other they each saw the Sun dancing on the shining body of the other.

They understood they were of the Sun and the Sun was of them.

Full with this wonder they fell to the sands again, until the Sun drew their spirits up to it and Sun filled them.

When night fell Sun sent their spirits back to their bodies, so they might wake and know of the Sun in the world, of the Sun that remained even in the dark. Sun showed them the little lights of the night so they would not feel lost and cut off.

They took food and water from the forest then, but they didn't go far for still they hungered for the Sun.

They ate and drank. They looked at each other again, and, again, each saw the Sun in the other. They came together to share their sun substance and each filled the hunger of the other, until the Sun rose anew and called them.

So it went the next day and the next until they were filled full with the Sun. On those days the Sun taught them their sun songs, so later they could share them in the forest darkness and remember the Sun.

After three days they were filled so full with the Sun that they could hold no more in their bodies. They returned to their people in the forest. There they sang their sun songs until the people began to awaken to the true light, and, finally, one or two at a time, they also hungered and reached for the Sun.

It happened that a baby grew in the belly of Nolak. It was not long after their journey to the Sun that she felt it growing, so she knew the baby came from the Sun. It shone, like every child shines, with the light of the Sun. The people marveled to see and treasured it, understanding that it came from the Sun.

When I finished the chant, I reached for the baby, He had been crying throughout my chant, and still he cried. I wanted to hold him close, to try to comfort him as his parents had been trying to comfort. And I did, for a moment, his skin against my skin, but then I held him up and out to the circle of the people, saying what we always said, "Gather to you this child of the Sun."

Babies wake and cry, but then they are comforted. Arms hold them safe and warm like the womb that held them, like the forest holds us, but Atoya cried and continued to cry, not loudly, but so sadly, fretfully, and he would not be comforted.

Messengers

The Messengers stayed with us for a time. They asked so many questions. Always they questioned and never revealed. Always calm voices and composed faces, except when, perhaps, they thought themselves hidden in darkness. Then their faces might take on a sad or brooding look, or the troubled look Doctor had had, or, more frequently, a look of irritability at the forest as if it oppressed them. The forest seemed always to be closing in on them. I would try sometimes to feel as they seemed to feel, imagine that the trees were pressing inward. For just a moment I could do it, then the forest returned to its familiar shape.

There was more than that about them, though. Sometimes I felt a hunger in them, beneath their calm words. It seemed almost constant, yet not strong enough to propel them to whatever would fill it. I wondered whether they were truly blessed, or rather like the people of the old times, who lived in the light and so never saw it. Whenever I thought these thoughts I felt afraid for the baby, Atoya.

One day Loren and I sat in a little space I had cleared at the end of a path. Loren, of all the messengers, was the only one who managed to look at home sitting cross-legged on the floor of the forest, though his long vigorous limbs seemed to always be demanding more space in which to move. I leaned back against a massive tree trunk, one of the old ones said to have been there before the Sun made the forest grow so thick. New trees grow their trunks quick and thin in their effort to shoot up towards the Sun. Near this ancient tree, leaning back this way, I could feel myself a part of it, connected through it to its leafy branches swaying free under the Sun.

"Tell me more about these rashas," Loren was saying.

I tried to explain, "We hunger for the Sun, and the Sun calls us. If you live always in the Sun perhaps you don't know of this?" But, as always, he ignored my question and told nothing about himself or the place he was from.

"How many have you had?"

I grinned at him. "Fourteen," I said, "more than anybody except old Lokla." Then I added quickly, "But that doesn't include my first time when I traveled to the Sun behind my mother on her sun path."

I told him about that time with my mother, how she taught me things I needed to know to let me serve the people during my rasha time, how to start a fire from the dead branches on the sand - for in the forest we can not light a fire lest it choke us. I tried it again and again through the night until I could do it without fail. On the last night she showed me how to go among the nisa and other animals that had not yet wakened from sun trance and choose the males or older females to kill so their spirits might stay joined with the Sun. She showed me how to slit their throats quickly, then to cut out the sun organ, for it would be wrong to eat of the sun substance of another. Then she had me light the fire to cook them by, and I felt very proud when I succeeded because now I could bring the people a rasha feast.

Loren leaned forward, resting his chin on his knees. He looked so young. Perhaps he missed his home. It must be so far. Nobody nearby had such light skin and hair, or was so tall. I felt like putting my arm around him, but somehow I felt I shouldn't do that with the messengers. Maybe that was part of their hunger - they didn't seem to touch each other. It might have been a good thing if I'd followed through with my feelings for once. How can I explain it? What seemed so easy and natural with us was hard with them. He was so inside, inside his own skin, as if he never left it.

I held back, felt awkward. Maybe I gestured towards him. That was all.

But then Loren said, "Could you tell me about them?" And then I was taken aback at being asked. Nobody asks about another's sun time. You can choose to share it, but it is the most private thing we have, and raw, without protection. And here this man with whom I didn't even share a touch, wanted to share that. I felt I should be angry, but I wasn't. He radiated such a need that it overcame any other feeling that I had. So, I tried to tell him what I could without weakening the power of my memories.

"I hunger for the Sun," I began. My voice was halting. I was not used to sharing this. "Then I must go. There is nothing in me but my hunger, no other thought but the yearning for the Sun. I press my way out of the forest, breaking or cutting through the growth however I can. It takes a long time, but the Sun calls to me and gives me the strength to come to it. Finally I reach the Sun shore, and my body falls on the sand while my spirit flies up to the Sun.

"I can't tell you of that. We don't speak of it except to those closest to us."

Loren nodded that he understood, but when I looked at him, he glanced away. Was he disappointed, hurt? Whatever he felt one moment he would hide the next. He'd ask another question, maybe.

But now I tried to give him more without him asking. I didn't want to hurt him.

"When night comes the Sun sends me back to my body, and I go to look for food and water in the forest. But I don't go far because it is hard to leave the sun shore at all before my hunger is satisfied. Two, or maybe three nights I stay on the shore. On the last night I can return quickly because my path is not yet grown over.

"On the first nights, as soon as I have eaten, I sing my sun songs. Some of these songs are just given when I am with the Sun. They are in my head fully formed. Others don't come until I begin to sing. It is as if I am releasing songs that have always been in me.

"Usually there are others there too, and when they sing their songs we find each other. Sometimes we simply stay together, singing through the night. Other times I have found someone. We see the Sun in each other and go off by ourselves to make love and spend the night together."

"With a stranger?" He looked shocked, but quickly tried to hide it.

I laughed. These messengers were so odd. The things that shocked them, or didn't bother them at all, it was so strange. Then I was afraid I had hurt him again, but no, he smiled a little.

I told him, "The Sun can join even strangers together." Tala had been a stranger met on the sun shore. And then he wasn't.

I tried to explain, "It is different then. People are different. You see them differently, as if you are seeing their center, the place where they are one with the Sun."

I told Loren more stories about my times on the sun shore, but I kept to myself my memories of what happened when I was with the Sun. Still, whenever I mentioned the joining with the Sun, an odd look filled Loren's face. It seemed a kind of yearning hunger. He asked, "Is everyone called?"

"Yes, everyone," I answered him. I was too astonished to say anything more. It shook me much afterwards too, this thought that someone might not be called to the Sun. What kind of people held such fears?

Tala

Tala had been on the sun shore with Miriac. Miriac was from my tribe also, and she was my lover.

Miriac had gone into rasha, and it had set me off as well, so that my rasha came the next day. That night I found her. She was beautiful, of course. She was always beautiful, but it was like I could see inside her that night. She was laughing, talking to this young man sitting across from her. He had the darkest hair. He seemed so alive. His face responded to everything that she said. Watching him with her, it made me feel like I had ignored her up to then, only half listened, not seen.

Then she had noticed me and had looked straight at me. At once I felt that she had seen everything about me. Perhaps, she too, had not really looked at me before then. She smiled, and I smiled back. I moved near them.

"This is Tala," she said. "We met last night."

I turned to him. Our eyes met, and then it seemed like time stopped for a little while. Finally I said, "Hello."

He laughed. It was as if I had said something clever. It was silly. Yet it was not silly, because it was as if we both knew that this was the beginning of things for us. How did we know? I don't know. But I knew. I love Miriac. She was beautiful and honest and clear. We've known each other since childhood. But just a moment with Tala and I knew that he was going to be something more to me.

He started singing. This was not unusual. During the day the Sun gives the songs. In the night we sing them to teach each other. Tala's voice was high and clear. Miriac began a song at the same time and it was different and yet it wound in and out with Tala's song, and somehow they both worked together as if they were layers of one another. I began with my song, and as I sang I felt it change to go with theirs. It was my song but it grew and became more than my song. This was something special, something I hadn't experienced before on the sun shore. We sang without stopping for so long that second moon appeared then rose in the sky. It was full, its pink halo shown very clear. As we sang we reached out and held each other's hands so that instead of three people in a circle, we sang as one person. All of a sudden we all stopped at once.

Miriac fell back and lay on the sand. And I lay down beside her and rested my hand on her belly. Tala lay on the other side of her, and he took my hand so both our hands rested on her. We lay like that for a while, comfortable. The three of us have always been so at ease with each other. It was as if Tala, too, had been a childhood friend.

But just a little later I leaned into Miriac and began kissing her lips. Tala laid his head close, and I began kissing his lips as well. Then I held back so that Miriac and Tala could kiss. For a while we only kissed. Then both of us, Tala and I, began touching Miriac's body, beginning with her breasts, and then moving all over caressing her. I remembered Tala kissing and sucking on her breasts, while I used my fingers between her legs, and felt her response at first subtle and slow and then increasing. As her hips began to rise and fall rhythmically I moved lower and began using my mouth and my tongue. Her hips moved up faster, then down, and I moved along with her. Then I felt Tala, pulling at my clothes.

I had never before made love with more than one person at a time and I have never since. But that night our bodies were so intertwined as if almost, we shared one body. My clothes lay on the sand. A tongue licked at my nipples. Hands reached for Tala's loincloth and pulled it away. Fingers traced my chest, along my belly, my abdomen. A penis swelled and rose up, then another. One was mine, which one? A vulva slid over a penis. It seemed my vulva, my penis. We rose and fell together. Hands cradled hips, buttocks, and pulled them down, a quick thrusting, then let them rise. Sensations, small pleasures in my vagina, my penises, and my lips touching lips, tongues touching tongues, teeth nibbling nipples. I would be kissing, lost in kissing, as if there were nothing else, and then my awareness grew to my whole body, to all our bodies and beyond them. When we came, it was as if we exploded outward into everything.

We lay back and watched the stars, the two moons, but for a while they did not seem to be stars and moons, but markings on a distant skin that enveloped all of us.

Finally, we slept for a time, before day came and we were filled with the Sun again.

The three of us spent another night together, but on the last night it was only Tala and me. Miriac had been filled with the Sun and gone. The two of us lay that night quietly together. That day our spirit had been joined in the Sun. We rested by drinking each other in through the night. I knew it was Tala with whom I wanted to share the same sun path. I gathered my courage and spoke to him. I hadn't known how scared I was until I heard his answer.

Tala said, "Yes, I want that too." My fear broke then and left me trembling. Then I felt my spirit soar as if it would reach the Sun once again.

Tala had no children of the tribe from which he came. So he left me for a little that night while he journeyed back to his people to

27

tell them that he was leaving. I lay in the dark at the edge of the forest waiting for him to return. It was strange how I felt, afraid that he might think better of it and not come back. And at the same time I felt confident that he would return and that my life would begin in a new way.

He did return, and that's how it happened that both of us were father to Miriac's child, along with her other lovers from our tribe. It was this girl-child who was later the mother of Nochi, Nochi, who is now mother of this strange great-grandchild, Atoya.

Tala and I continued to share our sun times until the time came when the Sun called Tala to it more and more frequently. And then he went, and did not return.

Loren

Loren seemed especially interested in that, how Tala went more and more often to the sun shore.

"Does that always happen before someone dies?" His face looked bright and eager. Then he hesitated. "I'm sorry. Perhaps you don't want to talk about it."

"It's okay," I said, and it was. It had been so hard to be left behind when Tala had gone, and to see him so weak, and not to know if he would return. And when he didn't return, all my memories of him came and went in my mind like little scenes. He was so alive in those memories. It did not seem possible that he could be gone. And I felt angry. How could I be? And yet I was angry. How could he leave me? I wanted to yell it out. I broke through the forest far from our dwellings and I did yell it out, "How could you leave me?" Just as if I had not seen him weakening day after day. As if he had chosen, and had walked away from me. But he did walk away. He was with the Sun when he died, not with me.

I answered Loren, "It happens often, but not always. Sometimes people die suddenly, clutching their head or their chest as if in pain, maybe falling. They might die right away, or, in a day or two. There are illnesses that kill in a few days, or a week. But, often it happens as people get old, they go to the Sun more often."

Then I stopped.

"But Tala was not that old," I said.

We should have had longer together.

Then all Loren's questions were about how often the rashas came, and how much they increased, and how many died when they were not yet old, and how did I know that Tala was sick, exactly. Exactly, always he wants exactly. Did Tala have a fever, trouble breathing, lose weight? And how old was old?

There is the deepest darkness of the year, and that is followed usually by the rainiest time. Even in the rainiest time, here in the forest the rain does not pelt down upon it, as rain comes down on the sun shore, but the air feels moister, and the bark of the trees feels wet. Moisture gathers in places, turning the dirt to mud. And, we can hear it, far above us, as it hits the leaves up there, sometimes loud, but distant, then letting up. It gets a little colder in the night in the darkest time, but not by much, and the dark is not so much darker. The light seems to come from different directions at different times, but it is not that clear since we are not able to see the Sun inside the forest. I don't think I noticed it much at all when I was younger, or, it was just the way the weather varied from time to time. As a child it took awhile for me to be aware that there was a pattern to it. The adults would speak about it. They'd talk about a child born in the rainy season, or the dark season, or the light season. Or about something that happened the year the dark stayed longer.

Loren asked me much about the change of seasons, how we tell.

He asked me how many rainy seasons had come in my life. But I had not counted. So, he asked how many times for a rasha. I had to think, and tell him that they were not so exact. The intervals were sometimes longer or shorter, though about the same. I hadn't thought of counting that way. But I guessed the rainy season might come five times.

"And you," I asked, "How many rainy seasons have come in your life?"

He told me it was different where he had been born. There wasn't a season that was wetter than the rest, although there was one that was hotter, and then it didn't rain as much. He said they kept a closer track on time, and always knew how many days, months and years had passed. He told me the meaning of months and years, but I wasn't clear how they knew it was their moon going around their earth that made it look like it changed its shape. I tried to follow his explanation, but I'd barely begun to imagine it in my mind before he'd gone on to another topic.

I wonder about him, Loren, because they left just a few months after Atoya was born. I had got used to him. I'd even looked forward to his silly questions. I thought he'd brought a difference to the forest, a little difference, I'd thought, not enough to be disturbing.

Rasha

I saw the sun hunger come on Atoya. I knew what it was, but it was strange, because he didn't begin breaking and hacking through the forest. Instead his body was overcome by a strange twitching. Then he threw himself on the ground and began flailing wildly and crying out. I had never seen a rasha like this before. Then Nochi, my granddaughter, appeared, deep in her own sun hunger. Calling to Atoya, she began chopping away. But Atoya didn't follow her, neither hacking his own small path, nor following behind on hers. I was dreadfully frightened for him. I went over to him to pick him up off the dirt.

"Come, boy, you must go to the Sun." As I said this, his limbs struck out at me, and the boy seemed unable to hear. His mother had turned around. I could feel her agony, wresting herself against her own Sun hunger to stop and look for her child. What could I do? One cannot follow another's sun path, except a small child going with its mother. Each must make their own way to the Sun. I couldn't follow behind Nochi with the boy.

Yet, there was Tala, my partner, there in the face of the mother looking back at me, and in the child at my feet. It was as if Tala, and through him the Sun, called to me. So I shouted to Nochi, "Go on, I'll bring the child." Released, she turned her head. Then a wild blow of the child struck my forehead so I felt angered for a moment, even knowing he was not responsible. But my anger passed. I wound my arms around Atoya to restrain him as best I could, and followed after in his mother's path. I couldn't help and hold the boy at once so it was both monotonous and tiring, without the extra strength that came with being in rasha. After a while I didn't hold him at all but merely pushed him along in front of me. From time to time I tried to show him what he should be using his limbs to do. Atoya only flailed like before. He was still flailing hours later as we neared the beach. When I shoved him out of the path and into the Sun he ran several steps aimlessly. Then he collapsed, exhausted into sun trance. I gave thanks and skirted away out of the reach of the sunlight. Then I fell and slept for some hours before making my way back.

Atoya returned with his mother a few days later, the twitching and flailing stopped, but he seemed no better to my eyes. His look was aimless and he seemed shamed by something he didn't grasp. I called to him, and he came.

"Well, child, you have seen the Sun."

"Yes, Poppa."

But why this uneasiness if he had met with the Sun? I wanted to ask Atoya what had happened, but that was a question one doesn't ask even a child. But Atoya looked up at me, and answered the question I had not asked, "Poppa, my sun body wandered and wandered, searching on the sands. It did not go to the Sun. The Sun did not call me. Why not, Poppa?"

I couldn't answer. I was stunned. The Sun always called. How could this be? I gathered Atoya in my arms and held him close.

The boy had been strange from birth, but he was worse after his return. His anger was greater and he seemed filled with a vague kind of helplessness. He struck out at the other children. Only his lack of force or direction prevented one of them from being hurt. Still, he had to be watched, lest even his aimless blows hit someone by accident. The other children began to avoid him. He never entered into the games of the forest, never cut through the forest with a crude axe or knife, pretending he was in rasha making a path to the Sun, never entered the vine climbing games to see who could climb nearest to the Sun. Sometimes he would hang about the very youngest children, watching them as they played with those who cared for them, as if there were something there that he wanted but didn't know how to reach. Even those tiny ones could use their muscles better than Atoya could, were already testing themselves on hanging vines, and scurrying to the forest after an older girl or boy, breaking through what twigs and roots they could and still keep up.

I felt desolate after Atoya's return. I'd been counting more than I knew on this first sun time of Atoya's to somehow right things. Now, as I looked out at Atoya, seeing not a small child anymore, but a half-grown boy, I felt not just desolation, but intense fear. It would be time soon for Atoya to have another rasha, and this time he would not be with his mother. He must make his way to the sun shore himself. How could he manage it? What would happen to him if he didn't? I didn't know. I stared out at Atoya with great intensity as if I could see him more clearly, to find some answer in him. And then Atoya's movements did begin to make some sense to me. For the thought came to my mind, fully formed and with certainty, "He is trying to be born."

Nochi's Story

It was a dry time. Even in the morning there was barely dew on the leaves, unlike other times, when the plants would almost drip with it, and the air felt heavy with moisture. I like these dry times when everything feels sparser. The edges between things get a little more distinct. It all blurs in the damp.

But I was getting big and waiting was harder when I could see the unborn child swimming within me whenever I lay upon my back. The child would move, and the bulge would go from place to place. I used to steal away so I could lie back and pull the clothing away from my big belly and watch. Not that anyone would be put off by the sight of my body, but somehow I wanted to be alone to watch and speak with this being inside me.

I didn't have a name for the child to be born yet, but I felt it, a dreamy sort. This might be a child to take things in slowly, but completely, as if becoming what is seen for a time. This one, I might need to guard a little more than children usually were guarded. Well, that's what I felt, but I also told myself to wait and see. What can you tell about a fish swimming about in your stomach? Maybe this feeling came from me and not from the little fish at all.

But I lay on the ground, rubbing my belly, caressing the skin above the lump, and speaking to it.

"Hey, little one, who are you?" I asked.

I had swept together a mound of fallen leaves within the makeshift shelter of two interwoven saplings bent together, and they rustled beneath me. I imagined sounds forming into words. But I couldn't quite tell what they were saying. I imagined the baby forming words, but indistinctly. They would come clear later.

Yes, I was impatient for this baby to come.

But they came, those Messengers. I was with Grandfather when they appeared. First one came out. He was dark in his face and his hair was brown like ours mostly is, but the rest of him was covered with so much clothing I could not see more, except his hands, which had five fingers like ours. He looked so strange I counted them, as we count the fingers and toes of a new-born child. But I could not see his toes. His feet were covered.

When he stepped out, and then another, and another, I felt my hands go to my belly as if to protect it. Perhaps my hands knew something I could have remembered later.

I let Grandfather do the speaking. Anyway, I was mostly inside myself, the time was close for the baby to come. I did not feel like coming out to talk with these strangers. I drew back into shadows where I listened and watched, but they may not have even seen me then with their eyes unused to dark. I could see that, the way they hesitated and stumbled.

Then the light came on. It was so bright. Grandfather shouted out. I didn't shout. I stepped out of the way so it could not touch me. There was something scary about light within the forest. Grandfather asked them how they brought it, but they only shut it off and did not answer him. They pretended it had not happened, as if they were allowed to play with the light, but not us. Yes, it scared me, and then I felt angry. What right did they have to bring this light, to scare me, and then to shut it off again? Who were they?

Did I think they were something special to have the light when we did not? Maybe, I don't know. Was that why I allowed them to take charge? I don't know. I had gone inward. I was holding myself steady, ready, open for the child to come. It was not my time to act on the world.

The strangers seemed so certain of things.

Oh, little one, I felt you coming. It was the next evening when I felt it in my belly, the tightness for a moment, that came and went. Only later, closer together, did it turn into a pain. I started building the hut. It is easier in the dry time when the branches come off the trees more easily. I was making a stack of twigs, pulling down the vines from which I would bind them together. The harok bushes had a soft leaf that I would spread over the ground to receive the baby when it made its way out.

I was ready to begin weaving when Kalak came to me. He touched me, but I didn't stop at first. He touched me again before I realized. I looked at him.

He looked worried. "They say you should stop," he said.

"They?"

"The strangers. They say it could harm the baby. They say you should rest."

Harm the baby? A part of me wanted to scream out that they were idiots, and scream at Kalak too for saying such a thing, as if we didn't know how to welcome a baby into the world, as if I would harm my baby by building a place for it. But Kalak looked so uncomfortable, shifting from one foot to another, waiting for me, so my anger faded.

"What do they know?" I asked him. I glanced over at them. They sat on the forest floor, but they weren't comfortable there. Kalak was not comfortable. Even Grandfather. But they had light.

"But they had light," Kalak echoed my thoughts. "Don't worry, we'll build the birthing hut. The baby will have a place to come.

"What do you think?" he asked me.

They had light, but my body wanted to move. But Kalak is afraid. I feel his fear, even the strangers' fear I can feel, and Grandfather, even he is not calm. I want to calm them. The baby should not come into an uneasy world. And it is this way with the fathers. The child comes from us, from the mothers. It is ours. This is clear. But the child becomes of the fathers as they care for the mother and welcome the baby into the world. Sometimes, perhaps, the baby is from the sperm of one of them. Sometimes, later, the resemblance is strong enough that we think it is so, but more often it is not. So we try to honor the fathers by accepting their care and their love.

So, I agreed. I went to sit against a nearby tree, and to watch instead of build. That was the first wrong step. But how could I know then? Then I just concentrated on my breath, to calm myself and calm the baby. I spoke to the baby about the place they were making for it, so it would be protected when it came out into the world. When the pains came I followed them in my mind so I would not cry out. In between I felt the baby move and I thought it was getting ready for its journey as well.

But it was a mistake, because then once the hut was built, the one called Doctor took over. I went inside with Kalak, and Grandfather and the Doctor came after.

"You should lie down," Doctor told me. I don't know why I did it. I didn't feel like lying down. I felt like walking round and round the bed. But I lay down. Maybe he'll leave, I thought, and I can get up later.

But instead he brought out that thing and made the light again. My eyes closed to shut it out, at first. It seemed brighter in the hut than it had been when it spread into the forest. I was not used to light. The bright light of the Sun on the shore is what puts us into sun trance. The light made me feel I was half in a dream. I was overwhelmed. I laid my head back on the pile of soft leaves on the bed, and I felt as if events were carrying me along. I was not in control.

When the doctor told Grandfather, and my other lovers, Rian and Sofelt, to go, I didn't protest. And then I just did what he said. He put his big hand on my belly, and pressed down along it, and I let him. He had me bend my knees and spread my legs far apart. He put a finger inside of me, then another. "Two centimeters," he said, "almost three." I am amazed that I let him touch me so, but somehow then I didn't care. He showed me how wide it was, how wide a centimeter was and two and three.

Then a long time went by. And through all of it there was the light, and there was Doctor with his hands on my stomach and his fingers inside of me, measuring the opening with his spread fingers, and each time when he announced the width, his voice a little more worried. Finally, I just longed for it to end.

Did I let my impatience get the best of me?

I don't know. It felt so oppressive. How could I not think it was bad for the baby as well, and when Doctor said it was taking too long, it was bad for the baby, I remember, I agreed. It seemed long, so long, all the waiting. I thought, let it end now. He said he would cut the baby out, but it wouldn't hurt me. He would stop the bleeding quickly. I didn't even care about how. Yes, just do it, I thought. And did I even think what it would be like for my baby to be lifted out into all that light? Did I even wonder how it would change things if the baby didn't make its own way out of my womb?

I should have wondered. I should have said no. I should have gotten up off that bed and told Doctor to leave so I could walk and wait for the baby to come in his own good time.

Atoya, I am sorry.

Atoya's Story

I used to like to listen to the stories that the grownups would tell at night with the children all gathered round. It used to be that I would sit there with the other children and I'd be able to sit, for a time, because I really wanted to hear those stories, but then I'd get restless. I'd feel like everything was crowding in on me. My arms and legs felt like they were twitching inside, and I'd have to get up and walk around.

I guess when I was really little, I didn't really notice the others looking at me, and I didn't really notice the noise I was making, so that the storyteller's voice got louder so people could hear. Sometimes Mama, or Poppa, or one of my fathers reached towards me, and I'd go over to sit in their lap for a while. Then I'd be up again. Nobody made me stay still. Nobody said anything to me about it. But I got older and then I could feel them looking at me. I could feel them wondering why I always had to disturb the story. Still, nobody said anything, and it was like the vines and twigs in my face. I wished they would say something. And, if they had, perhaps I would have screamed at them. But they never did, so I started to leave the circle, and go out on the edges and listen from there while I walked back and forth, or around the circle, and always looking in from the outside.

And then, then I went to the Sun.

Nobody really says much about the rashas. But you know it is special. You see people going. They make such a commotion, even more of a commotion than I made, when I just had to get up and be moving. Then they would come back a few days later, and everyone was glad to see them. They bring food with them, different food.

41

And they glowed. That's how it seemed to me, that they glowed, that they were stronger, healthier, more beautiful.

I wanted to go.

Well, everyone wants to, not just me. All the games are about rashas. All the kids, except the very littlest, have axes they've made themselves from stone and wood. Nobody makes one for you, but the grownups will show you anytime. I know how. I've memorized it. You find a rock, and another smaller rock. The black rock is best. It is gray on the outside, but black and smooth and shiny when broken open. It isn't hard to find one that has already split so the shiny inside already shows. You find a place where there is a right angle or close to one. You knock the loose pieces off the bigger rock with the smaller one just to clear them away. Then you pick the spot where you will hit hard to knock loose a chip. You keep at this until you have a chip that is big enough and sharp.

Now you use your smaller stone to work the chip. First you hit softly along the thinner edge breaking off the brittle sharp little pieces that aren't strong but could cut you. You use the same motion along the edge to shape it. You might switch to a piece of bone now to hit smaller pieces and make it smooth. Sometimes you grind the small stone along the other to smooth it too, and grind to leave what is left very strong. If it is an axe you will want it sharp on both sides, so you have to thin it by knocking flakes off the thicker side and then working it to a sharp edge. Only the side that will touch the wood is left blunt. You imagine a center to the piece, and the edge is there at the center. You flake pieces off the side to keep it symmetrical. You flake off very small flakes to make a serrated edge. Finally, you make notches on either side to be able to tie.

You can use this tool in your hand to cut a handle from a tree branch, but you don't need to, because there are usually old axe handles about that you can use. There is a special type of vine that makes the best rope when we pull out fibers and then roll them together to make a strong rope. This is what we use to tie the axe to the handle.

It all sounds simple, doesn't it? But it is hard to do it right. For everyone the rock flakes wrong, or breaks in two, but then, finally they get it. Then they are able to make a good blade nearly every time.

But not me. I never did. All my rocks broke, all of them. The grownups would tell me to take it slower, make little chips. But you don't understand. I couldn't go slower. My body wanted to fly apart and start running. I couldn't sit there. I'd throw the rock and start hitting the branches with my fists. I'd break through as fast as I could to get away from my failure. When I calmed down - when I'd gone so far that I was too tired to go further - I'd fall on the ground, and then I'd think about the rock with the sharp edge that someone might cut themselves on. So, I'd go back, but the rock was never there. Someone had already put it aside somewhere safe. I'd want to hide then. Again someone had cleaned up for me, made sure I didn't hurt anyone. I was ashamed of my outburst. But when I asked to be shown again, a grownup always showed me. They never told me to remember the last time. But I remembered, and after it had happened so many times, I felt too ashamed to ask again.

I was little then, though. The next day would be a new day, and I didn't think so much about the knives. In a way, I'm not sure I thought so much at all in the way I described it. Those thoughts probably came later when I came back from my rasha and remembered, but I know I felt different. I felt wrong. And I hoped for something, that my rasha would come. I would go to the Sun, and the Sun would make it right.

I can't talk about that now. I can't. It hurts. It still hurts.

There was one story I especially liked. I don't know why. It seems an odd story for a little kid to like, but there was something about it.

The story is about a man and a woman, grownups. They belonged to different tribes and they did not know each other. But one day they both went into rasha, at nearly the same time. Separately they felt the need for the Sun. The strength of their need filled them, and they made their way to the sun shore. They reached the shore and burst into sunlight. It happened that they ran out both at the same moment, and they saw each other at the same time that they saw the Sun. As their tired bodies lay on the sand their spirits rose and joined with the Sun.

But in the mind of each was that vision of the other, that instant when they saw. When night came and the Sun released them the man, whose name was Neblan looked around for the woman. She was near, just coming out of her sun trance when he found her. They spent that night together, and the next. Every moment they were not with the Sun they were with each other.

But then the last night came. They stayed together until almost dawn. They talked and talked. Neblan asked the woman, Dasa, to come with him that night, to walk his sun path home. She thought of leaving all her people and she could not. She told him, and asked him to come with her. But he could not bear it either. They parted. They told each other that they would meet again, and perhaps the next time.

He went home. She went home. She was all he could think about, and he felt such a fool not to have gone with her. It would be so long before another rasha and who knew if their days would come together a second time. He decided to start looking for her in the forest. It happened sometimes that two tribes ran into each other as they moved their camps to look for food. Not often, it didn't happen often. Two tribes could pass very close to each other without knowing the other was there because the forest was so thick. But if he were looking, she could be very close.

At the same time Dasa was having the same thoughts. Now that he was out of her sight, she could think about nothing else. No one else felt as important to her. She struck out on her own cutting paths to search for him.

They were both out there, all alone, searching. They never knew, but a few times they came very close to each other, but passed without realizing the other was there. For years and years they were alone, except for the brief companionship they found on the sun shores when their rashas came upon them. They searched on the sun shore as well, but either their rashas did not come together again, or they had emerged in another place on the long shore, and though Dasa would spend the whole night walking on the beach she never came upon Neblan.

It is a sad story, isn't it? But I changed it. I found someone on the sun shore on my first rasha. Not a woman, but another boy. And this boy was like me. I recognized that instantly, and so did he. Each night we ran along the shore together and swam in the warm shallow water. But on the last night, we were too young. We had to follow our mothers home. And we did, but both of us began to search for each other. We cut paths whenever we could into the forest, and one day, long after, when I was old enough to make my own way, I came upon a path I hadn't made. I followed it, first one way until it ended, and then the other. And there he was, sitting in a clearing. His face

45

when he saw me was so happy. No one had ever looked at me before with such happiness. We were friends, and we never left each other again.

I used to imagine this boy so often; I could picture him so clearly, his dark hair, his eyes that tracked so quickly, and the smile that lit up his face. Whenever I was out walking I'd be imagining him and our adventures together.

Sun

Once I'd been shocked when Loren, asked me if everyone was called to the Sun. But now? The Sun had not called my great-grandson, and I, who loved him, had robbed him of his birthing journey. I had been wrong. My thoughts of a special destiny had been wrong. Does the Sun choose one child over another? I realized I had known all along the wrongness of it, known it was not the Sun but something else that had drawn me then. The weight of this lay heavy on me. But what could be done now? I had thought the Sun would welcome Atoya, would bring him within, let him see that he was part of the Sun and of all things, that there was no reason to stay on the edges anymore.

Could the Sun really have turned on my great-grandson? I could not believe this. The Sun was there for anyone who hungered for it, only somehow Atoya was not able to reach or recognize it even as it filled him. For a while, too, I had worried about my sacrilege and following in my granddaughter's sun path.

I was afraid that I might have angered the Sun against Atoya and perhaps it would turn the Sun against me as well. But on my next rasha I had been put it ease, for the Sun had not turned from me. As always I'd merged with it, and later my memory of it was even stronger than it had been when I was younger. Even within my sun trance I felt myself questioning. Why had they done this thing, those travelers from another world? Why had the Sun let it happen? Why was my great-grandson not called to the Sun? I felt the Sun's presence there, listening, patient at my restlessness. The answer: not in words, only, "Everything, everything is here within me. Everything is home."

"But why?" I kept asking, and this the Sun did not answer.

I kept asking after I had returned to the forest. Was it to teach this new thing, this restlessness, this flailing without purpose, this anger without direction, this problem without solution? What was the Sun trying to teach us?

"Everything is within me," so the Sun had answered. So then everything, my great-grandson, the travelers, their tampering with Atoya's birthing, all this must be a path to the Sun too. How was this path followed? How could I teach the boy to follow it, my great-grandson who had not truly been born?

So I wondered again and again, urging Atoya to join the games and the storytelling at night, and having the child turn from me, or move away to the edge of the circle. Until I wanted to grab and force him though that was not our way, nor the way of the Sun, which was to let things come in their own time.

Now this day I had watched the boy come into the clearing and realized that his rasha time was coming soon, and he must make the journey to the Sun on his own. But what if Atoya could not make his way through the forest? What if he spent his energy thrashing on the ground?

I was startled out of my thoughts by the sound of a nisa breaking and slithering its way to the brambles and roots of forest. "I shall meet you in the Sun, little brother." It was an automatic thought, yet it heartened me. For I believed it was true that Atoya too, for all his strangeness, was of the Sun and would return to the Sun. If this was so then the strangeness and fear and pain were all of the Sun as well and the way must be found to let the Sun shine through them. A way would be found. I thought, "He needs to birth himself." I puzzled over that, for how could Atoya birth himself now? Yet I came to the decision and next day I began work on a strong knife and axe for Atoya.

Rebirth

When they were ready I called Atoya to me. The boy came sullenly as he did now. I was not a man who forced another to his will, but I persisted. "Atoya, you must learn to cut a path through the forest so you will be ready when the hunger comes."

The boy looked ashamed, turned and dropped his head, "The Sun does not want me."

"You are part of the Sun, Atoya. You must make your path to the Sun. I've made you a knife and axe. You must practice making paths through the forest with them so you will be ready when it is time to make your path to the Sun."

"Poppa, the Sun doesn't want me. It didn't call me. It let me wander on the sand," he was almost crying out the words.

I answered quietly, fervently, "Perhaps it was because you didn't make your own way to the beach, because I had to push and carry you there. Maybe the Sun wants you to carve your own path to it. Come, let's practice, so next time you will know what to do."

The boy cried out angrily, waving his arm over towards the little ones, "They know what to do already, only I don't. Why am I so different? The Sun doesn't want me. Practicing will make no difference, the Sun still will not want me."

Now I too yelled in anger, "Then do it anyway. You can do no harm."

I seized the boy's hand and put the knife into it. Atoya pulled away from me and thrust the knife away, so the tip of it grazed the skin of my leg, stinging and drawing blood. I almost struck him in a fit of rage, and started to shake him instead.

I drew back from him, trembling. What was I becoming?

Well, now I'd felt Atoya's rage and helplessness. Perhaps he could feel something of me.

But Atoya stared, white-faced, stricken, at the blood trickling down my leg.

"It is nothing," I said, and brushed the blood aside. Then I handed Atoya the axe and said, "Will you take it, or will you cut me again?"

He just stood there, unmoving, with the axe in his hand, holding it at arm's length as if in terror of it. I put my hand around Atoya's wrist and swung it, saying, "You chop this way."

The boy did not chop, but he let his arm be swung. So I swung it, until I was too weary to swing more.

The next day the boy was compliant no longer. He refused to take the axe or the knife. He wouldn't close his hand about them. So I put the knife in Atoya's hand and forced his fingers about the handle. But as soon as I let go, he didn't fling the knife but simply let his fingers drop open and the knife fall. So I put it back in his hand and closed his fingers around it again, and this time did not let go. I swung Atoya's arm so the blade sliced, and said, "This is how you cut through the forest," until the boy resisted, trying to hold his hand still against me.

So we struggled, me, an old man, my arms thin and trembling with exhaustion, and the boy, tightlipped, holding himself rigid, his eyelids almost closed in his attempt to remain immobile. Me, the old man, thinking, "Force is not the Sun's way. This cannot be the path to the Sun," yet still pushing, pushing, in some stubbornness I had not known I possessed.

The boy seemed to be thinking only, "I won't," and holding himself rigid against me, the old man, until finally it grew too much for him and he let his arms go limp and flailing once again, so I, the old man, was taken by surprise and stumbled forward. Then the boy dropped the axe and lashed out with his fists, hitting whatever was in the way, a tree, roots, me. He hit without direction, without much force.

It was only then seeing him act as he usually did that I realized he'd been different that morning. In his defiance the boy had seized some purpose he hadn't had before. He had stopped flailing and held himself firm against me.

So I thought, happily, "Well then, fight me if you must." I wondered how this could be the way of the Sun. Yet I felt that it was, the way somehow twisted and turned on itself, yet still the way.

But the struggle went on for days, many rounds of days. Every day Atoya fought me. He was sure of his purpose while I tried to hold on to mine. I could imagine his thoughts, imagined him asking: what does he want from me? I imagined him calling me a bully, like some two year old who tries to push other children around. I imagined him thinking, that I, too, had turned against him.

I repeated my words mechanically, straining to believe them, "Swing this way, Atoya. This is how you make your way to the Sun."

"There is no Sun," Atoya yelled at me. "There's only the dark."

My arm stopped swinging.

52

"But you've seen the Sun."

"Maybe I just dreamed it," Atoya said. "I was little then."

It was not that I had never doubted. There were times when I'd thought it was all the workings of a sun-parched mind that threw up what I needed. There'd been times that I felt so parched - when Tala died was such a time - that it was hard to believe there was anything beyond loss.

But as a boy, Atoya's age, then I had simply been full of everything. I felt the connectedness of it all, without thinking of it. I lived within the tribe and the tribe nourished me. The world was full of kindness for me. There was always someone ready to hold me, someone who would comfort if I needed it. Every child was a child of us all.

It was only age and death that came and made me feel that it might not always be enough.

No one had turned on Atoya. They all still taught him patiently although Atoya had such trouble learning. Yet even that seemed to grate at him. He was like those others, the messengers, who came but never looked at peace.

"No, Atoya. It wasn't a dream. The Sun is there and you will find it." My voice sounded certain. I wondered where that certainty came from.

The only thing that gave me hope was that he didn't run away from me when I went to get him. He never resisted until I had put the axe in his hand.

The rest of the tribe stayed away from us as we struggled, and did not comment.

One day, Atoya screamed at me, "Why are you doing this? Leave me alone. Just leave me alone." He was crying.

And there was Nochi, looking on. She looked at me. I felt the question, "Are you sure?" I met her eyes, and shook my head slightly, no, and made a gesture of helplessness, meaning, but what can I do?

Atoya went on, "I'm different. Don't you understand? I've always been different."

I saw the hurt in Nochi's eyes as she moved out of sight. Atoya didn't seem to have noticed her.

I said, "We are all different, Atoya. But you are still a part of us." He just hung his head as if despairing of me, deciding that I would never understand.

Atoya Speaks

I am different. Don't you understand? I've always been different. I watch them. I am outside. The others are home here. The forest loves them. The vines that hang down are the toys of the little ones. They swing on them. The older kids walk through them as if they don't feel their tickling, or they play a game of swinging them to another boy or girl who swings them back. Sometimes there are two vines and they keep it up in a rhythm, back and forth, and they sing as they do it, in time with the swing. Or someone swings on one, knowing they are too heavy and it will break. At the moment it breaks they make a leap and land gracefully on cleared land, or in a nest of soft growth they've chosen beforehand. They are full of grace. I am not.

I would like to say it, in words. I want to ask, "Doesn't the forest hurt you?" I want to say. I want to explain. It hurts me. But how do I explain it. It is like a continual noise that is too loud. It is as if the touch of the forest cuts me, although it doesn't in a way that I can show, but that is how I feel it. It is as if every step that I take that should be inside, is outside instead, and I am always outside.

I have to go. I have to find a place to rest that is somewhere on the edge. Sometimes if I find a clear place where I can stand and hold on to something, something steady, then I can just stand there quiet and it can be okay for a while. Except then the dark comes deeper and the place that is cleared feels smaller, closing in on me, and then I feel that I must go ahead, and walk and walk, and thrash out, and get it off me. I want to scream out, but if I scream out, they will come as they did when I was smaller and couldn't stop the screams. They picked me up and asked me what it was, and then

55

there were all these touches like the vines, the flowers, the weeds of the forest always touching, and I screamed, but I could not tell them that they hurt me. They pressed me in, and I needed to go free.

Yes, I know they love me. They hurt for me. That is what I am, the one who causes pain. When I am looking from somewhere hidden I see them relaxed, at ease. But when they see me, when Mama looks at me, when Poppa looks at me, there is always worry on their faces. When they see my sister, Lauril, it is different. Their faces light up. I want to be the one that makes them happy, but I am not. I am the one who brings them pain and worry. That is what I am and all I am.

Rebirth, Continued

Another day Kaleb came, watching from nearby. His body was tense but he didn't intervene. At times he'd put his arm up against his ears as if he didn't want to hear, but he stayed. I knew he was watching out for his son. Once Atoya looked up and saw him there. His face went white. I could see the thought, "They've all turned against me now."

But that was how he'd always felt, wasn't it? No, not quite, he'd trusted us, although he felt apart.

Atoya's face had taken on a hard look. His resistance was more determined, pushing my hand away.

"Ok," I said, "that is enough for today. We will start again tomorrow."

"You think we will start tomorrow."

The next morning when I went to look for him he was nowhere. What will I do? I thought, fearfully, before I remembered myself. I would do what we always did when a child was missing. I strapped the axe to my belt so my hands would be free and set off to look for him. It was not hard. Atoya did not walk lightly. Vines were broken, leaves shoved aside. I thought he might climb, though Atoya had never been a good climber, but when I found him he was sitting on a pile of moss and leaves, sweating and exhausted. He'd been building a hut, not carefully made, just branches heaped together.

"It won't stay up," he told me. "I can't do anything."

"No," I said. "We'll have to start over."

I dragged the branches off to one side. I pointed out one of the larger ones, and told Atoya, "Let's start with that one."

Atoya started to drag it and it was clear that he had exhausted himself before I got there. I grabbed a part of it and together we hauled it into place. But I, too, had worn myself out the previous day. We let the branch fall and sat down.

I looked over the rest of the pile. I found a branch that would work and used the axe to trim the leaves and twigs from it. Then I handed over the axe, and pointing to another good size branch, asked Atoya, "Can you do that one?"

Atoya hesitated, but he took it.

"Stroke away from yourself, " I reminded him.

Atoya did, and when we had stripped a few, I told him we would need some long vines. So Atoya cut and I showed him how to weave the pieces together.

I decided that this would not be a small child's hut. It would be a proper hut that Atoya and I would build.

"When I was a little older than you," I said, "I wanted a private place where I could go and be alone and think."

"You?" said Atoya, "But I thought you liked to be with the others?"

"Yes, I do, but not all the time. Sometimes you need to be alone to be who you are meant to be. Anyway that was how I felt."

"I don't know if there is anything I am meant to be," said Atoya. It hurt to watch him with the shame and doubt in his eyes.

I said. "You don't have to know it all at once. You can try something out, and later try something else.

"Today you are a builder," I said, and he looked a little better.

Atoya regained his energy before I did, so I set him to clearing away a larger space and stripping the limbs from the small trees he removed. Together we bound several trunks together to make the corner posts and we dug into the ground with our knives to make a hole for each to sink into.

All day we worked hard, breaking off to gather some food and eat, or an occasional rest. I needed it more than Atoya. I had never seen him work so hard to accomplish something.

It was impressive when it was done, not very wide or long, but sturdy with a ceiling high enough for Atoya to stand, and the walls filled in tight. We'd even made a door that he could swing to close himself in.

And better, as I'd watched him work I'd realized that he had become more skillful with his tools. He swung his axe deftly and he'd gotten stronger.

"Will you stay here tonight?" I asked him.

"Yes, " he said. Then he looked at me. "I helped you today, didn't I?"

"I helped you," I said. "You did most of the work."

He relaxed then. His face grew soft, and he smiled.

I said, "I'll let Nochi and Kaleb know you're spending the night here. I'll see you in the morning." I was ready for my own sleeping place.

And then, next day, it was as if it had never happened, that day of working together. Now, we were fighting again. I had convinced myself that we would be friends now, but it didn't happen.

The only change was that he no longer flailed. He grew stronger, holding himself against me.

One day I was unable to move Atoya's arms at all. So I let go, and said, "Okay, you have won. I cannot force you any longer."

Atoya looked up at me in surprise, then a look of triumph passed over his features.

We stood still for a moment, and then I spoke again, "I can't force you, so you must do what you want to do."

He did not move or speak. I think he didn't breathe. It was only a moment, maybe, but it was so long. Then he breathed. He breathed again, more deeply, and his body relaxed. It was like watching him as a newborn when he took a breath and turned from blue to pink.

He said, "I will make a path."

So he made paths, and I, the old man, showed him again how to hold the knife and axe, and how to make the strokes to cut most easily. We worked together now.

Once the boy asked me, "What do I do now if I make my Sun path and still the Sun does not call me?"

"I don't know, Atoya. Perhaps if the Sun does not call to you, then you must shout after the Sun asking why it does not take you when you are part of it, and it is part of you. I am no longer sure of the ways of the Sun. I only know that there is a Sun, and there is a path for you to reach it."

Looking at Atoya now, I saw that part of him coming clear that was Tala and yet not Tala. Atoya could laugh now, but his laugh was not Tala's. It was his own.

"He is birthing himself," I thought, "and so am I."

A few days later, I came upon Atoya, thrashing again, flailing again, wild.

I picked him up, but I could not get him to stand. He fell and pounded the dirt. Again and again I lifted him, grabbed hold of his arm.

"Atoya, Atoya, please stand up."

Time and again I grabbed around his chest and lifted, and he became a dead weight, striking his own feet out from under himself. He hit out with his arms, at anything, at me.

Had it all been for nothing?

He pulled me down with him. I struggled to my feet and once again pulled him up to his. I'm not sure where the strength came from.

He struck out. Then Atoya was not just flailing, but striking out more forcefully. I fended him off. He was stronger. His blows hurt me even as I fended them aside.

I tried to grab his arms and called to him, "Atoya, Atoya, listen, go to the Sun."

My strength was running out. His had grown and seemed to be growing still.

Finally, I picked him up one last time. He broke free of my hold and his hard young fist caught me on my shoulder.

I am ashamed to admit it, but my frustration was so great that I struck him back. At once I was horrified at what I'd done, but I had no time to think about it because now he turned on me and fought. All his strength was now directed at me. It was all I could do to hold him off.

I kept shouting, "Make your sun path."

Finally he seemed to hear and turned towards the forest. Then I, the old man, pulled my axe out of its holder. I shoved its handle towards Atoya. I was afraid he might yet grab it and come at me. But he took it and headed toward the shore.

I watched him, watched for a long time, till the boy's path curved and I could see him no longer, nor follow.

Song of the Hayak

We are of the Sun.

We always have been.

We were in the light and we did not know.

No more

Now we know the light even in darkness.

The dark teaches us of light.

The dark leads us to light.

I look at you and I see the Sun there

in the heart of your dark mystery.

Do I remember it truly?

It has been long since that last rasha time.

At times I question -

Did the Sun truly call me,

really take me in?

Song of Atoya

I am Atoya

who came into the world with no birthing journey.

I did not know how to meet the forest

with my struggles caressing her.

I thought I should sit in the dark of her branches in shame.

I was not born,

not until my grandfather came forcing me into the birth passage

bearing down on me to make my way to the Sun.

I fought him. I learned to fight like a lover.

I hit him when he touched me,

but that did not stop him touching me softly in my middle

until I ran out of the forest to the Sun.

Let me be born, I cried.

Why did you leave me behind?

The Sun took me.

The Sun answered.

I never left you behind.

Only then I realized it had always been everywhere.

Once I walked off balance.

Now I dance.

It is still hard sometimes.

You have never known this, have you, you others?

You have never known what it is to be on the outside,

to linger at the edges

longing to be one of the unselfconscious ones, laughing and playing.

I wonder do you ever think such thoughts,

but you know, you always belong.

The Sun never let you wander unanswered on the sand.

Why me?

Why have you not spoken to me? I ask,

until finally I feel it, I hear it; all along we have been speaking

together, underneath the noises of my brain.

I had not noticed.

There are simple steps beautiful in their simplicity,

and there are steps that come clear and simple at last.

Does it matter which I step?

I don't know.

To dance is good.

www.ingramcontent.com/pod-product-compliance
Lightning Source LLC
Chambersburg PA
CBHW071203130626
46555CB00004B/1570